W9-BTL-623

A Nice Party

Withdrawn

Elle van Lieshout & Erik van Os

Illustrations by
Paula Gerritsen

Front Street & Lemniscaat
Asheville, North Carolina

"Why so gloomy, pal?" Boris asked.

Gus sighed. " Oh, tomorrow's my birthday," he said.

"Your birthday! How could I forget? We'll have a grand party!"

"Oh, no, not a party. See, that's just it. My family always throws the worst parties.

"My grandmother squeezes me
and tickles my belly and kisses me
and pretends I'm a baby bear,"
Gus complained.

"And my uncle always shakes
my paw and says, 'You'll be quite
a bear someday, my boy.'

"And my two cousins always eat
the whole cake before I can even
make a birthday wish."

Just thinking about it made Gus sad.

"Hey, I have an idea," Boris said.

"Let's go fishing—just you and me. We'll take a cake and bring our fishing poles and stay by the river all day."

The bears posted a note for Gus's family—

Dear family,

Thanks for coming to my party. I'm sorry I couldn't be here. Please leave presents by the tree.

Kind regards,

Gus

The next day, Boris burst through
the door singing Happy Birthday.

Then the two friends walked to the river.

Gus's family didn't notice that Gus
was missing. His cousins played with
the new soccer ball that his grandmother
brought. His uncle played the guitar
and sang, "Gus is quite a bear."
The bear family ate up all of the
cupcakes and made a mess.

After everyone left, Gus's aunt stomped away, grumbling, "Gus didn't even show up for his own party."

But Gus didn't mind. Not one little bit.